22518

DATE DUE

Top 10 Big Men

Chris W. Sehnert

ABDO & Daughters
Publishing

Published by Abdo & Daughters, 4940 Viking Drive, Suite 622, Edina, Minnesota 55435.

Copyright © 1997 by Abdo Consulting Group, Inc., Pentagon Tower, P.O. Box 36036, Minneapolis, Minnesota 55435 USA. International copyrights reserved in all countries. No part of this book may be reproduced in any form without written permission from the publisher.

Printed in the United States.

Cover and Interior Photo credits: Allsports Photos
            Wide World Photos
            Bettmann Photos
            Sports Illustrated

Edited by Paul Joseph

Library of Congress Cataloging-in-Publication Data

Sehnert, Chris W.
   Top 10 Big Men/ by Chris W. Sehnert
      p   cm. -- (Top 10 Champions)
   Includes index.
   Summary: Covers the careers and statistics of ten NBA big men:Hakeem Olajuwon, George Mikan, Bill Russell, Wilt Chamberlain, Willis Reed, Kareem Abdul-Jabbar, Dave Cowens, Bill Walton, Moses Malone, and Bill Laimbeer.
   ISBN 1-56239-794-X
   1. Basketball players--Biography--Juvenile literature. [1. Basketball players.] I. Title. II. Series: Sehnert, Chris W.
   Top 10 Champions.
   GV884.A1S45 1997
   796.323'092'2--dc21   97-2106
   [B]   CIP
                         AC

Table of Contents

George Mikan

Professional basketball is a game dominated by *Big Men*. In the NBA (National Basketball Association), often the smallest man on the court is taller than an average-sized human being. The biggest man on any given team, more often than not, plays the position of "center." He is responsible for controlling the area beneath the basket. On defense, the big man protects the goal, swatting away shots from close-in and gathering rebounds off the glass. Offensively, he is a high-powered weapon. Lurking in the lane, with his back toward the basket, the center awaits a teammate's pass before spinning and powering his way for a field goal.

The first big man to dominate professional basketball was George Mikan. At six-feet, ten-inches tall, George's great height advantage was responsible for several rule changes that exist to this day. He led the Minneapolis Lakers to four NBA Championships in five seasons. He retired as the NBA's all-time leader in career points (11,764), points in a season (1,932), career scoring average (23.4), and scoring average in a season (28.4). More than 40 years after leaving the basketball floor, George Mikan's name has been replaced in the record books. His legend as basketball's first superstar lives on.

George Lawrence Mikan, Jr. was born in Joliet, Illinois. His father taught his son the value of hard work from the time he was a boy. George began playing organized basketball at Chicago's Quigley Prep School. While attending Joliet Catholic High School, he suffered a broken leg. The injury restricted him to bed rest for all of 18 months and excluded him from competition. During the time of his

recovery, George grew eight inches, reaching six-feet, seven-inches tall by the time of his high school graduation. With no high school basketball experience, George was not afforded the luxury of an athletic scholarship. He enrolled at De Paul University, in 1942. Ray Meyer took over as head coach of De Paul's basketball team that season. Upon meeting George, Meyer quickly set out to develop the giant freshman's potential. The coach enlisted George in a workout regimen that included skipping rope, shadowboxing, using a punching bag, modern and ballet dancing, and 200 hook shots with each hand every day! George became a three-time College Basketball All-American, and led the nation in scoring in his junior and senior seasons.

George took his patented hook-shot to the professional ranks in 1946. He joined the Chicago American Gears of the National Basketball League (NBL). The Gears won the NBL Championship in George's rookie season, but the franchise folded under financial strain. The next season, George became a member of the Minneapolis Lakers where he was a unanimous choice for the NBL Most Valuable Player (MVP) Award, and led his team to a second-straight league title. In George's third professional season, the Lakers joined the BAA (Basketball Association of America). The results were again the same. George led his new league in scoring, and carried the Lakers to another league championship. After the Lakers' 1949 BAA Championship, the league merged with the NBL to form the NBA. George Mikan and his Minneapolis Lakers continued their domination, winning four of the first five titles in the new league. Regardless of the competition, one thing remained constant in the early days of professional basketball. If George Mikan was playing center, his team could count on winning it all. He established a legacy for basketball's *Big Men* to follow.

PROFILE:
George Mikan
Born: June 18, 1924
Height: 6' 10"
Weight: 245 pounds
Position: Center
College: De Paul University
Teams: Chicago American Gears (1946-1947), Minneapolis Lakers (1947-1956)

CHAMPIONSHIP

SEASONS

1946-47
NBL Championship
Chicago Gears (3) vs.
Rochester Royals (2)

1947-48
NBL Championship
Minneapolis Lakers (3) vs.
Rochester Royals (1)

1948-49
BAA Championship
Minneapolis Lakers (4) vs.
Washington Capitols (2)

1949-50
NBA Championship
Minneapolis Lakers (4) vs.
Syracuse Nationals (2)

1951-52
NBA Championship
Minneapolis Lakers (4) vs.
New York Knicks (3)

1952-53
NBA Championship
Minneapolis Lakers (4) vs.
New York Knicks (1)

1953-54
NBA Championship
Minneapolis Lakers (4) vs.
Syracuse Nationals (3)

George Mikan

UNFAIR ADVANTAGE

George Mikan was personally responsible for several rule changes, which big-men of today must follow. While he was attending De Paul University, the NCAA instituted the "goal-tending" rule. This prevented a player from interfering with a ball while it is in the imaginary cylinder above the rim. Later, the NBA began enforcing the "lane violation" rule, which prevents an offensive player from remaining in the foul lane for more than three seconds. To further limit George's effectiveness, the NBA widened the foul lane from 6 to 12 feet.

PEERLESS GEORGE

The Associated Press dubbed George the "Greatest basketball player from the first half of the 20th century." He was inducted into the Naismith Memorial Basketball Hall-of-Fame in 1960. In 1996, he was selected among the NBA's 50th Anniversary All-Time 50 Greatest Players.

George Mikan at De Paul University.

MR. COMMISSIONER

George spent his off-seasons studying law at De Paul University, where he passed the bar exam. He later became the Lakers' General Manager and opened a law practice. In 1967, he became the first commissioner of the ABA (American Basketball Association), which would eventually merge with the NBA in 1977.

George Mikan approaches the basket for a layup.

STUBBORN AND DETERMINED

George Mikan's string of championships actually began in 1945 when De Paul University won college basketball's NIT (National Invitational Tournament). George scored 120 points in four games, and was named the tournament's MVP.

Being on a championship team eight out of ten seasons made George a target for his opponents. "It was constantly a test as to whether or not I was able to beat the other guy," George remembers. "It was a day-to-day type of competition. Every time I played, they wanted to beat me. But being stubborn and determined, I wouldn't let them."

Mikan, shooting his patented hook-shot.

Bill
Russell

"Defense is a science." With these words, Bill Russell explained his unique philosophy on the game of basketball. It is a belief that served him well. In 1980, the *Professional Basketball Writers Association* voted him as the "Greatest Player in the History of the NBA." This praise was bestowed upon a man with a less-than-lofty (15.1) career scoring average. What is undeniable, however, is that Bill Russell was the NBA's premier defensive scientist.

William Felton Russell was the second son of Charles and Katie Russell. He was born in Monroe, Louisiana. His father moved the family to Oakland, California when Bill was five years old. "I should epitomize the American Dream," Bill would later say. "For I came, against long odds, from the farthest back to the very top of my profession. I came from the Depression, from an oppressed minority—first in rural poverty and then from a city's ghetto. I had to persevere to succeed, to climb out of the life that society had

programmed for me. I was not immediately good at basketball. It did not come easy."

At Hoover Junior High School in Oakland, Bill failed to make the basketball team. He was growing fast, and was awkward on his feet. As a freshman at McClymonds High School, Bill barely made the junior varsity team, sharing the last uniform with another player. By his senior season, he had begun to put on weight and was gaining coordination. He was far from being a polished performer, but he was still growing.

The University of San Francisco (USF) offered Bill an athletic scholarship, after his high school graduation. It was a small school at the time, with little or no reputation for basketball. There Bill met K. C. Jones, who would become his teammate in college as well as in the pros. Together they brought the USF basketball program to unimaginable heights. In Bill's junior season (1954-55), the team started with four straight victories before losing to UCLA. It was the last defeat Bill Russell would suffer on a college basketball court. The next game, USF began an unprecedented 55 game winning streak, culminating in two straight National Collegiate Championships. Bill was the MVP of the 1955 NCAA Basketball Tournament, and in 1956 he was named college basketball's Player of the Year.

Red Auerbach was the head coach and general manager of the Boston Celtics in those years. After ten seasons in the league, the Celtics had failed to win an NBA Title. In 1956, Auerbach traded two of his finest players to the St. Louis Hawks, to acquire the rights to draft Bill Russell. In a short time, the Boston Celtics would set-forth on establishing the greatest championship tradition in the

history of professional basketball. Bill Russell's superior defensive skills turned out to be the missing piece in the Celtic's puzzle. Led by Bob Cousy, and later John Havlicek, Boston was a virtual offensive machine. With Bill pulling down rebounds, blocking shots, and quickly moving the ball up-court, they became unstoppable. The Celtics won their first NBA Championship in Bill's rookie season. They went on to win the league title 10 more times in Bill's 13 seasons as the Celtics' center. In 1959, Boston began a streak of NBA Championships that lasted eight seasons. Bill Russell, the NBA's scientist of defense was a virtual genius when it came to winning basketball games.

PROFILE:
Bill Russell
Born: February 12, 1934
Height: 6' 10"
Weight: 220 Pounds
Position: Center
College: University of San Francisco
Teams: Boston Celtics (1956-1969)

CHAMPIONSHIP

SEASONS

NBA Championships

1956-57
Boston Celtics (4) vs. St. Louis Hawks (3)

1958-59
Boston Celtics (4) vs. Minneapolis Lakers (0)

1959-60
Boston Celtics (4) vs. St. Louis Hawks (3)

1960-61
Boston Celtics (4) vs. St. Louis Hawks (1)

1961-62
Boston Celtics (4) vs. Los Angeles Lakers (3)

1962-63
Boston Celtics (4) vs. Los Angeles Lakers (2)

1963-64
Boston Celtics (4) vs. San Francisco Warriors (1)

1964-65
Boston Celtics (4) vs. Los Angeles Lakers (1)

1965-66
Boston Celtics (4) vs. Los Angeles Lakers (3)

1967-68
Boston Celtics (4) vs. Los Angeles Lakers (2)

1968-69
Boston Celtics (4) vs. Los Angeles Lakers (3)

THE SCIENCE OF DEFENSE

Bill Russell invented a style of defensive play which has become the foundation for the way 'big men' play the game of basketball. "Defense is a science," he said, "not a helter-skelter thing you just luck into. Every move has six or seven years of work behind it."

Bill learned that rather than just blocking shots, he could swat the ball in the direction of a teammate. When he came down with a defensive rebound, he became adept at throwing quick outlet passes. The Celtics continually out-scored their opponents by beating them to the other end of the floor and scoring easy baskets in transition.

Bill is currently second on the NBA's all-time list for rebounds, behind Wilt Chamberlain. Blocked shots were not kept as a statistic, until 1974. Aside from his 11 NBA Titles, Bill was named the league's MVP five times, and is considered the greatest defensive player in the game's history.

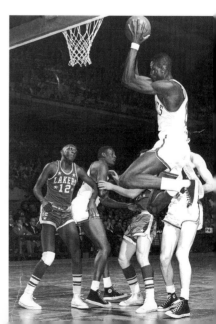

Bill Russell comes down with a rebound.

PLAYER/COACH

In his last three seasons as a player, Bill Russell led the Celtics from the bench, as well as on the floor. Red Auerbach retired from his coaching position after Boston's 1966 NBA Championship. His heir apparent was the man who guided the team to eight-straight titles. The Celtics were defeated in the playoffs by the Philadelphia 76ers in Bill's inaugural season as player-coach. He completed his amazing playing-career by guiding the Celtics to two more NBA Titles, in the next two seasons. He later coached the Seattle Super Sonics and Sacramento Kings.

Bill Russell goes for a layup.

SPEAKING OUT

Bill Russell became an advocate for the civil rights movement when his playing days were over. He traveled to college campuses across the country speaking his mind on many subjects, including race relations. "I am black, but I do not feel it incumbent on me to prove it by subscribing to any philosophy which requires that I cut myself off from all but my own race," he said. "I find that trend regrettable. People who restrict themselves to one race—who say they won't associate with blacks or whites, whatever the case—are only limiting themselves as humans. When you arbitrarily refuse to associate with another race, you are the loser, for you are going to miss out on a lot of beautiful people."

Bill Russell as coach.

Wilt
Chamberlain

Size can be a definite advantage to a basketball player. However, a height advantage alone does not guarantee success in the NBA. It must be combined with the qualities of strength and agility. These were the characteristics of Wilt Chamberlain. At seven-feet, one-inch tall, Wilt towered over his opponents. But, it was power and grace which left him standing above the rest in basketball history.

Wilton Norman Chamberlain was one of nine children born to William and Olivia Chamberlain. He grew up in Philadelphia, Pennsylvania, where his father worked as a handyman and his mother was a maid. His parents were both about five-feet, nine-inches tall. Wilt was an ordinary-sized boy himself, until the age of 14. Then, he began to grow, and grow, and grow some more! During a single summer he shot up over four inches, and by the time he reached high school, he was 6-feet, 11-inches tall!

Wilt began playing basketball at Shoemaker Junior High School. He also competed in track and field. He continued developing his talents in both sports while attending Overbrook High School. In his three seasons, Wilt led the Overbrook basketball team to a 58-3 record and two City Championships. He also became Philadelphia's high school champion in the high jump and shot put competitions.

Two-hundred colleges and universities from across the United States recruited Wilt for their basketball programs. Expressing an appreciation for Coach Forrest "Phog" Allen, Wilt chose the University of Kansas. In his sophomore season, he led the Jayhawks to the 1957 NCAA Finals, where they suffered a disappointing (54-53) loss to North Carolina in triple-overtime. Phog Allen retired before the next season, and Kansas did not make a post-season appearance. Wilt was continually triple-teamed by the zone defenses allowed in college basketball. Frustrated by Allen's departure and the rules of the college game, he left Kansas University after his junior season.

The Philadelphia Warriors of the NBA attained the rights to sign Wilt while he was still in high school. At the time, however, the rules of the draft made him ineligible for four years. With one season of ineligibility remaining, Wilt became a member of the barnstorming Harlem Globetrotters. Playing to sellout crowds around the world, he refined his skills in preparation for the big leagues. "They all want to see Wilt," said the Globetrotters owner. The next season, Wilt would begin his personal assault on the NBA record book.

As a rookie for the Philadelphia Warriors, Wilt broke eight NBA single-season records, including most points and most rebounds. He was honored as both Rookie-

of-the-Year and the NBA's MVP. From that point forward he continued to smash his own records. Beginning in 1960, he led the league in scoring seven straight times. Wilt was the league's leading rebounder 11 times in his 14-year career. In 1968, he became the only center to ever lead the league in assists.

The only things that prevented Wilt Chamberlain from piling up a bevy of championship trophies were Bill Russell and the Boston Celtics. Throughout the decade of the 1960s, the NBA Playoffs inevitably came down to a battle of these Hall-of-Fame *Big Men*. In all but one, the Celtics prevailed. In 1967, Wilt's Philadelphia 76ers finally broke Boston's eight-year stranglehold on the title. Wilt won one more NBA Championship with the Los Angeles Lakers in 1972. By then, Bill Russell had retired. But make no mistake, in the history of professional basketball, Wilt Chamberlain stands alone.

PROFILE:
Wilt Chamberlain
Born: August 21, 1936
Height: 7' 1"
Weight: 275 pounds
Position: Center
College: University of Kansas
Teams: Philadelphia Warriors (1959-1962), San Francisco Warriors (1962-1965), Philadelphia 76ers (1965-1968), Los Angeles Lakers (1968-1973)

CHAMPIONSHIP
SEASONS

Wilt wins a tip off.

1966-67
NBA Championship
Philadelphia 76ers (4)
vs. San Francisco
Warriors (2)

1971-72
NBA Championship
Los Angeles Lakers (4)
vs. New York Knicks (1)

HERSHEY'S
KISS

On March 2, 1962, the Philadelphia Warriors and New York Knicks met in a small arena at Hershey, Pennsylvania. It was in this regular-season contest that Wilt Chamberlain recorded his most outstanding individual achievement. Wilt had already set the NBA record for points in a single game (78), earlier that season. On this night, he would sink 36 field goals and convert 28 out of 32 free throws for an even 100 points. When his final two-point shot kissed off the glass and into the net, the Hershey crowd showered their approval upon him with an extended ovation. The Warriors won the game (169-147) as Wilt completed one of the most incredible accomplishments in the history of professional sports. Wilt's 50.4 scoring average that season is also the NBA's best ever.

GOLIATH

Basketball fans and sportswriters often referred to Wilt Chamberlain as "Wilt the Stilt." Reportedly, he despised the nickname, preferring to be known as the "Big Dipper." In spite of Wilt's overall dominance, at times he was booed by the crowds who watched him play. He explained his lack of popularity by saying, "I am Goliath and the world is made up of Davids. Nobody roots for Goliath."

*Wilt comes down
with a rebound.*

> *"I always loved the game, even if it didn't always love me."*

NBA LEADER BOARD
for Points in a Single Game:

	Date:	Pts:
Wilt Chamberlain, Philadelphia vs. New York	3/2/62	100
Wilt Chamberlain, Philadelphia vs. Los Angeles	12/8/61	78
Wilt Chamberlain, Philadelphia vs. Chicago	1/13/62	73
Wilt Chamberlain, San Francisco at New York	11/16/62	73
David Thompson, Denver at Detroit	4/9/78	73
Wilt Chamberlain, San Francisco at Los Angeles	11/3/62	72
Elgin Baylor, Los Angeles at New York	11/15/60	71
David Robinson, San Antonio at L.A. Clippers	4/24/94	71
Wilt Chamberlain, San Francisco at Syracuse	3/10/63	70

NBA Leader Board for Scoring Average in a Single Season:

	Season:	Avg:
Wilt Chamberlain, Philadelphia Warriors	1961-62	50.4
Wilt Chamberlain, San Francisco Warriors	1962-63	44.8
Wilt Chamberlain, Philadelphia Warriors	1960-61	38.4
Elgin Baylor, Los Angeles Lakers	1961-62	38.3
Wilt Chamberlain, Philadelphia Warriors	1959-60	37.6
Michael Jordan, Chicago Bulls	1986-87	37.1
Wilt Chamberlain, San Francisco Warriors	1963-64	36.9

ALONE AT THE TOP

Wilt Chamberlain held over 40 NBA records at the time of his retirement. He was named the league's MVP four times, and played in 13 NBA All-Star Games. Wilt remains as the NBA's all-time leading rebounder (23,924). His career points record (31,419) has only been surpassed by Kareem Abdul-Jabbar (38,387). Wilt currently ranks second on the all-time list for career scoring average (30.1), behind Michael Jordan (32.2).

Wilt above the rim.

Willis

Reed

Every so often, a player exceeds expectations to become an NBA superstar. Such was the case with Willis Reed, the Hall-of-Fame center of the New York Knickerbockers. The Knicks had the first selection in the 1964 NBA Draft. They passed on Willis, and so did every other team with a first-round pick. When the small-college star was still available in round two, the Knicks didn't miss their chance. Willis responded by becoming the NBA's Rookie-of-the-Year that season. He would later bring New York a pair of NBA Championships!

Willis Reed Jr. was the only child of Willis Sr. and Inell Reed. He was born in the village of Hico, Louisiana. His father was a truck driver and warehouse foreman. The family lived in the small town of Bernice, Louisiana. Willis grew strong at a young age, hauling hay and wheat for local farmers, cutting grass, and performing other odd jobs. By the eighth grade, he was already six-feet, two-inches tall, and like most oversized young men he was quite uncoordinated. It was around this time when he began to participate in athletics.

Willis attended Westside High School in the nearby town of Lillie, Louisiana. He was a member of the track and field team, and also played football, baseball, and basketball. "I wasn't good, but I was big," Willis would later say. When the Westside basketball coach, Lendon Stone, caught him dunking the ball in practice, he taught Willis a lesson he would not soon forget. "He yelled at me, 'You can't even walk yet and you're showing off. Why don't you do something constructive?'" Willis remembers. "From then on I decided I would learn to do everything with the ball that a little guy can do." He began building his coordination through hours of jumping rope and practice in the gym. As a senior, he was an all-state athlete in both football and basketball. He graduated with an above average academic record, and he had grown to six-feet, seven-inches tall.

Several NCAA Division I colleges and universities recruited Willis to play basketball. He was intent on staying close to home, however, and accepted a scholarship to Louisiana's Grambling State University. Grambling was considered a small college at the time, and was part of the National Association of Intercollegiate Athletics (NAIA). The Tigers' basketball coach had supplied Willis with sneakers for his hard-to-fit size 15 feet, while he was playing at Westside High School. Willis led Grambling to three Southwestern Conference Championships and the 1961 NAIA Title during his time there. He was named to the small-college Little All-America basketball team three times. More importantly, he had prepared himself for the next level.

The New York Knicks considered Willis among their top three candidates in the 1964 NBA Draft. The team's management was astounded to find him still available in round-two. Their excitement proved worthy, as Willis set a team record for rebounds that season, and led the Knicks in scoring. In a short time, he would become the team's all-time leader in both categories.

With the addition of power-forward Dave DeBusschere in 1968, the Knicks began climbing in the standings. The next season, they finished on top of the NBA's Eastern Division, and went on to win their first league championship. Willis was a three time MVP that season, accepting the honors for the league's All-Star Game, regular season, and for his performance in the NBA Finals! In 1973, Willis Reed was the MVP of the NBA Finals once more, as the New York Knicks completed their second championship season. He retired after the next season, and was elected to the Naismith Memorial Basketball Hall-of-Fame in 1981.

PROFILE:
Willis Reed
Born: June 25, 1942
Height: 6' 10"
Weight: 240 pounds
Position: Center
College: Grambling State University
Teams: New York Knickerbockers
(1964-1973)

SEASONS

Willis Reed (19) moves in to block a shot.

1969-70
NBA Championship
New York Knicks (4) vs.
Los Angeles Lakers (3)

1972-73
NBA Championship
New York Knicks (4) vs.
Los Angeles Lakers (1)

TEAM PLAYER

Perhaps the greatest contribution Willis brought to the Knicks was his ability to inspire great play from his teammates. With players such as Dave DeBusschere, Walt Frazier, and Earl Monroe on his side, that inspiration went a long way. "The intangibles about him are his drive, his desire, his defense, the way he blends his own game into that of his teammates, plus the way he gets the ball out quickly after a rebound," wrote Phil Elderkin. "By subordinating himself as an individual, he has made the New York Knicks a world-championship team."

A PAIR OF GIANT KNICKERBOCKERS

Willis Reed's status as the New York Knicks' all-time leader in points (12,183) and rebounds (8,414) has since been overtaken by Patrick Ewing. The seven-foot-center from Kingston, Jamaica, has been a member of the Knicks since 1985. Patrick led his Georgetown University basketball team to the 1984 NCAA Championship. He has yet to bring New York a third NBA Title. In 1996, both Patrick and Willis were named among the NBA's 50th Anniversary 50 Greatest Players of All Time.

MOVIN' ON

Willis Reed's playing career was cut short by tendonitis in his knees. He underwent surgery after a painful 1971 season, but the problem persisted. Willis played in only 11 games for the Knicks during their 1971-72 campaign. He returned the next season to lead the team to its second NBA Championship.

In 1977, Willis became the Knicks' head coach, and led the team back to the playoffs for the first time since his retirement. He was fired the next season after a disagreement with management over personnel decisions. He moved on to become the head basketball

Willis Reed goes in for a layup.

coach at Creighton University, and in 1987 he took over the New Jersey Nets head coaching job. Willis became the Nets' general manager in 1988, and in 1996 he was named the team's Senior Vice President in charge of player development and scouting.

Willis Reed chasing after the ball.

19

Kareem
Abdul-Jabbar

By the year 1967, Lew Alcindor had made a name for himself in the households of basketball fans around the world. The seven-foot, two-inch sophomore from the University of California at Los Angeles (UCLA) was just completing his first season of varsity eligibility. He led the Bruins to a perfect (30-0) record that season, captured the National Collegiate Basketball Championship, and was named the MVP of the NCAA Basketball Tournament. It was only the beginning. In the years that followed, Lew would lead UCLA to two more college crowns, change his name to Kareem Abdul-Jabbar, and spend 20 seasons as the most dominant center in professional basketball.

Lewis Ferdinand Alcindor was born and raised in New York City, New York.

He was the only child of Ferdinand and Cora Alcindor. Ferdinand was a police officer. Lew's parents were both slightly taller than six feet. He was an unusually large baby, weighing 13 pounds and measuring 22 inches at birth. By the age of 13, he stood six-feet, eight-inches tall and weighed over 200 pounds! Lew excelled in athletics as a young boy. He won trophies and medals as a swimmer, ice skater, and with his Little League baseball team. Before long, his great size led him to the basketball courts in and around New York's Central Park.

Lew soon became widely recognized for his basketball abilities and was recruited by several local prep schools. He accepted a high school scholarship to Power Memorial Academy, a Roman Catholic institution on the West Side of Manhattan. There, he became the basketball team's starting center in his freshman season. Following a rigid training schedule of skipping-rope, handball, and hours of work on the basketball court, Lew developed the coordination he would need to become a star. In his four years of high school basketball, he led Power Memorial Academy to a 95-6 record (including a 71 game winning streak), and three straight New York City Catholic High School basketball championships!

UCLA was a basketball power before Lew Alcindor arrived in the autumn of 1965. Under head coach John Wooden, the Bruins were the reigning NCAA Champions for two years running. Prior to 1972, college freshman were not allowed to play varsity basketball. In a preseason exhibition, Lew carried the UCLA freshman-team to a (75-60) victory over the varsity squad! In the next three seasons, the Bruins went 88-2, on their way to three more NCAA Championships.

During his years at UCLA, Lew was growing increasingly conscious of the plight many African-Americans faced. Before joining the professional ranks, he converted to the Islamic faith, and later, officially changed his name to Kareem Abdul-Jabbar. The Milwaukee Bucks chose Kareem as the first player selected in the 1969 NBA Draft. He became the NBA's Rookie-of-the-Year. The next season, he was the league's MVP and led the Bucks to their first NBA Championship.

Kareem Abdul-Jabbar played more seasons and scored more points than any man in the history of the NBA. In 1975 he became a member of the Los Angeles Lakers, where he stayed through the remainder of his 20 seasons as a professional athlete. With the addition of Magic Johnson, Kareem and the Lakers won five NBA Titles in the 1980s. He was a champion at every level of competition, and became a member of the Naismith Memorial Basketball Hall-of-Fame in 1995.

PROFILE:
Kareem Abdul-Jabbar
Born: April 16, 1947
Height: 7' 2"
Weight: 267 pounds
Position: Center
College: University of California at Los Angeles (UCLA)
Teams: Milwaukee Bucks (1969-1975), Los Angeles Lakers (1975-1989)

CHAMPIONSHIP
SEASONS

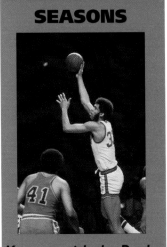

Kareem with the Bucks.

1970-71
NBA Championship
Milwaukee Bucks (4) vs.
Baltimore Bullets (0)
1979-80
NBA Championship
Los Angeles Lakers (4)
vs. Philadelphia 76ers (2)
1981-82
NBA Championship
Los Angeles Lakers (4)
vs. Philadelphia 76ers (2)
1984-85
NBA Championship
Los Angeles Lakers (4)
vs. Boston Celtics (2)
1986-87
NBA Championship
Los Angeles Lakers (4)
vs. Boston Celtics (2)
1987-88
NBA Championship
Los Angeles Lakers (4)
vs. Detroit Pistons (3)

SKYHOOK

As a college star Lew Alcindor struck fear into his opponents with his ferocious slam dunks! "He destroys you, that's what he does," said one opposing coach.

"Just his presence is a great psychological hazard," was the comment of another.

"He can hold you off with one hand and stuff the ball with the other. How are you going to stop him?" a third coach wondered. After Lew's undefeated sophomore season, the NCAA rules committee made dunking illegal in college basketball. The controversial rule remained in effect until 1976. There is little doubt it was made with Lew in mind.

Ironically, the dunk's prohibition was partially responsible for the development of another unstoppable weapon in the arsenal of Kareem Abdul-Jabbar. He called it the "Skyhook." Holding the ball high above his head before flicking it over a defender and through the net, the shot was virtually unblockable. On April 5, 1984, a Skyhook from Kareem moved him past Wilt Chamberlain for the most career points in NBA history!

Lew, slamming one home for UCLA.

AWARDS AND HONORS

1967- College Basketball First Team All-American
1967- College Basketball Player of the Year
1967- NCAA Basketball Tournament Most Outstanding Player
1968- College Basketball First Team All-American Center
1968- NCAA Basketball Tournament Most Outstanding Player
1969- College Basketball First Team All-American Center
1969- Naismith Award Winner
1969- College Basketball Player of the Year
1969- NCAA Basketball Tournament Most Outstanding Player
1970- NBA Rookie-of-the-Year
1971- NBA Most Valuable Player
1971- NBA Finals Most Valuable Player
1972- NBA Most Valuable Player
1974- NBA Most Valuable Player
1976- NBA Most Valuable Player
1977- NBA Most Valuable Player
1980- NBA Most Valuable Player
1985- NBA Finals Most Valuable Player
1995- Elected to Naismith Memorial Hall-of-Fame
1996- NBA 50th Anniversary 50 Greatest Players of All-Time

Kareem scores for the Lakers.

Kareem waits for a pass.

NBA RECORD BOOK

Most Seasons:
Kareem Abdul-Jabbar   20
Most Career Points:
Kareem Abdul-Jabbar   38,387
Most Seasons, 1,000 or more Points:
Kareem Abdul-Jabbar 19
**Most Career Blocked Shots
(compiled since 1973-74 season):**
Hakeem Olajuwon   3,190 (through 1995-96)
Kareem Abdul-Jabbar   3,189

Dave
Cowens

The Boston Celtics have the greatest championship tradition in the history of professional basketball. In 1969, Bill Russell's retirement signaled an end to a period of prosperity, in which the team won the NBA Title 11 times. Gone were the days of the fast-breaking, defensive-minded Celtics who wore out their opponents with sheer stamina. But not for long. After a season in which Boston missed the playoffs for the first time since 1950, Red Auerbach drafted a relatively unknown center out of Florida State University. Dave Cowens was smaller than contemporary pivot-men such as Kareem Abdul-Jabbar and Willis Reed. He made up for his lack of size with

tenacity and aggression. By 1976, Dave had helped hoist another pair of championship banners to the rafters of the Boston Garden.

David William Cowens was the second of six children born to John and Ruth Cowens. He was raised in Newport, Kentucky. The Ohio River Valley, which runs through the town of Newport, is a hotbed for basketball talent. Like nearly all of the other kids in the area, Dave grew up on the asphalt courts of the city's playgrounds. When he was in fourth grade, he joined the St. Anthony Elementary school team. His coach remembers Dave not for his ability, but for his competitive edge. "He was the type of boy who never wanted anyone to get the best of him in anything," he recalls. It is a description that would fit Dave's entire career.

Dave gave up organized basketball to join the swim team when he reached Newport Catholic High School. He also participated in football as well as track and field. He grew six inches during his sophomore year, and the high school basketball coach couldn't help but notice the six-foot, five-inch redhead. He convinced Dave to join the team, and put him in the varsity starting lineup in his junior season. Dave practiced hard to improve, and in his senior season he carried the team to the Kentucky State High School Tournament. Newport was defeated in the opening round, but Dave's skill as the teams leading rebounder drew the attention of college recruiters.

Dave received scholarship offers from several Ohio Valley schools such as Louisville and Cincinnati. In the end, he was most impressed by the growing basketball program of Florida State University. There he enjoyed a successful college career, but was rarely seen by the nation's basketball fans. The team advanced to the NCAA Tournament in Dave's sophomore season, but was eliminated in the first round. In the next two seasons, Dave was among college basketball's leading rebounders. The NCAA had placed the Seminoles on probation during those years. They were ineligible for post-season play and banned from national television due to some previous recruiting violations. It did not prevent professional scouts from taking notice of Dave's

abilities, however. In 1970, the Boston Celtics were looking for a player to step into the mighty shoes of the recently retired Bill Russell. They chose a fiery Kentucky-born thoroughbred. Dave was the NBA's Rookie-of-the-Year that season. Two years later he became the league's MVP. Using quickness and speed, he out-maneuvered his larger opponents, racing for loose balls, diving to make a steal, and leaping to reject their jump-shots. One observer reported, "If there were an NBA record for floor burns, it would certainly belong to Dave Cowens." In 1974, he out-dueled Kareem Abdul-Jabbar in the NBA Finals to bring the Celtics their twelfth championship and first without Bill Russell. In Dave's final season with Boston, he would pass the 'Celtic torch' to another future Hall-of-Famer from the Ohio Valley named Larry Bird.

PROFILE:
Dave Cowens
Born: October 25, 1948
Height: 6' 8"
Weight: 230 pounds
Position: Center
College: Florida State University
Teams: Boston Celtics (1970-1980), Milwaukee Bucks (1982-1983)

CHAMPIONSHIP SEASONS

Cowens blocks out Kareem.

1973-74
NBA Championship
Boston Celtics (4) vs.
Milwaukee Bucks (3)

1975-76
NBA Championship
Boston Celtics (4) vs.
Phoenix Suns (2)

RED SEES RED

Arnold "Red" Auerbach was the head coach of the Boston Celtics from 1950 to 1966. Since that time he has been the team's president. In 1980, he was selected by the Basketball Writers Association of America as the "Greatest Coach in the History of the NBA." In 1970, the Celtics failed to make the playoffs for the first time in Red's career, and the team's 'brain trust' took it upon himself to find their next great star.

Following the advice of Bill Russell, Red traveled to Florida State University to see Dave Cowens. "He was so good, he scared me," Red recalls. "There were scouts from a half a dozen other NBA teams at the game, and I figured if they saw the same potential in him that I did, we'd never land him. I kept hoping he'd make a mistake."

In an effort to throw the other scouts off track, Red left the game with five minutes remaining, pretending to be disgusted. Upon returning to Boston, he called head coach Tommy Heinsohn and told him, "Tommy, we've found the kid we want!" Dave was the Celtics first-round draft choice that season, and the fourth player taken overall.

26

Dave Cowens for the Celtics.

CELTICPRIDE

The Boston Celtics have won more NBA Championships than any other team (16). From 1946-1995 they played their home games on the parquet-floor of the Boston Garden. The team moved into the new FleetCenter for the 1995-96 season.

Of the 74 NBA players and coaches currently inducted in the Naismith Memorial Basketball Hall-of-Fame, 13 were members of the Boston Celtics. The list includes Dave Cowens, Bill Russell, Bob Cousy, John Havlicek, K.C. Jones, Tommy Heinsohn, Bill Walton, and Red Auerbach. Joining them in the near future will be Kevin McHale, Robert Parish, and Larry Bird.

Dave Cowens.

PASSING THE TORCH

According to Red Auerbach, the history of the Boston Celtics can be divided into three great dynasties; those of Russell, Cowens, and Bird. Following in the tradition of Bill Russell, Dave Cowens became the Celtics player/coach in 1978. The experiment lasted only one season. He returned to play one more season in Boston before retiring in 1980. After two years off, Dave played one final season as a member of the Milwaukee Bucks. In 1996, he became the head coach of the Charlotte Hornets.

R-E-S-P-E-C-T

Dave's father was a barber and store manager, who taught his children the value of respect. "He was a good model," Dave says. "No one could ever say a bad thing about him. You've got to do your best for yourself and those you're working with. You have to have respect for yourself and everybody else. It all comes down to the same thing, in sports, your job, school, anything."

27

Bill Walton

What does a long-haired, bearded vegetarian from California have in common with a Hall-of-Fame basketball champion? Answer: They're the same person. Bill Walton is considered one of the greatest college basketball players of all-time. In his first two seasons as the UCLA Bruins' starting center, the team did not lose a single ball-game. Bill's 14 season NBA career was a roller-coaster ride of highs and lows. Plagued by recurring knee problems, he missed four entire seasons and saw only limited duty in three others. While he was healthy, he led the Portland Trail Blazers to their first and only NBA Championship. Bill's basketball career ended as the league's top substitute, helping the Boston Celtics win their sixteenth and most recent NBA Title.

William Theodore Walton III was born in La Mesa, California. His father, Ted Walton, was a district chief in the San Diego Department of Public Welfare. Gloria Walton, Bill's mother, was a librarian. Bill has an older brother, Bruce, a younger brother, Andy, and a younger sister, Cathy. "I never tried to steer my kids into sports," Bill's father says. "I encouraged them to play, but only as a broadening experience, to complement their music. So wouldn't you know they all gave up music and wound-up in sports." Bruce Walton played three seasons as an offensive lineman for the Dallas Cowboys. On the high school basketball court, he played "blocking back" for his taller, much thinner younger brother.

The Walton brothers attended Helix High School, in San Diego, California. During these years, Bill had difficulty keeping his weight in step with the fast pace at which he was growing. By his junior season, he was a frail six-feet, seven-inches tall. When opposing basketball teams tried to rough him up or wear him down, big brother stepped in to help. Bruce was six-feet, five-inches tall, and 100 pounds heavier than Bill. "When the referee wasn't looking," their mother recalls, "Bruce would give the player an elbow and let him know that the skinny guy was his kid brother." In his senior season, Bill had begun to adjust to his size. He led Helix through a perfect (33-0) season, averaging 29 points and 24 rebounds per game.

Bill's outstanding performance as a high school senior left him with several options for college. He chose to attend UCLA, where his brother was playing football and where John Wooden had coached the basketball team to four-straight national championships. The Bruins won their fifth in a row, while Bill was playing for the freshman team. He became a first team All-American as a sophomore, as UCLA continued a winning streak that would smash the previous NCAA record. After two undefeated seasons and a seventh-straight national title, the Bruins were finally defeated in Bill's senior season. Notre Dame's (71-70) triumph ended coach Wooden's untouchable string of victories at 88 games. North Carolina State defeated UCLA (80-77, 2-OT) in the NCAA Final Four that season, ending the Bruins record string of championships.

Bill Walton was named basketball's College Player of the Year in all three of his varsity seasons. The Portland Trail Blazers made him the first player selected in the 1974 NBA Draft. With expectations at

their highest level, Bill began to struggle. He blamed his performance on a series of nagging injuries, while ruthless fans deemed him a "social misfit," based on his appearance and counter-cultural belief system. In 1976, Jack Ramsay took over as the Blazers' head coach and pronounced himself a "Walton Man." Bill was named Portland's team captain that season, and directed the team's new fast-break offense all the way to an NBA Championship.

Nine years after his first league title, Bill Walton found new glory as a bench player for the Boston Celtics. For the first time in his professional career, he remained healthy through the entire 80-game schedule. He received the NBA's Sixth Man Award, as the Celtics completed their sixteenth championship season. The NBA's official representative of the American Counter-Culture was elected to the Naismith Memorial Basketball Hall-of-Fame, in 1993.

PROFILE:
Bill Walton
Born: November 5, 1952
Height: 6' 11"
Weight: 235 pounds
Position: Center
College: University of California at Los Angeles (UCLA)
Teams: Portland Trail Blazers (1974-1979), San Diego Clippers (1979-1984), Los Angeles Clippers (1984-1985), Boston Celtics (1985-1988)

CHAMPIONSHIP

SEASONS

Walton goes up for a hook shot.

1976-77
NBA Championship
Portland Trail Blazers
(4) vs. Philadelphia
76ers (2)

1985-86
NBA Championship
Boston Celtics (4) vs.
Houston Rockets (2)

BRONTOSAURUS BILL

At nearly seven feet tall, Bill Walton might be the biggest vegetarian to walk the earth since the Brontosaurus! "I used to eat a lot of hot dogs and ketchup and french fries and steak and junk like that," Bill stated upon being questioned about his eating habits. "I know what *that's* like . . . . This is definitely a lot better."

THE WALTON GANG

The UCLA basketball team was nicknamed "the Walton Gang," after Bill's undefeated sophomore season. "It is mainly because of Walton's many talents that his UCLA team has landed with almost as much impact as the Alcindor sophomores of five years ago," William F. Reed wrote in *Sports Illustrated*. "The Waltons run a devastating fast break and they work Wooden's famed full-court press better than any UCLA team since the Goodrich-Hazzard-Erickson era [of the mid-1960s]."

Bill Walton led UCLA to many victories.

HARDWOOD HARDWARE

A Listing of Bill Walton's Basketball Awards:

1972- First Team College All-American

1972- College Player of the Year

1972- Naismith Award Winner

1972- NCAA Basketball Tournament Most Outstanding
      Player

1973- First Team College All-American

1973- College Player of the Year

1973- Naismith Award Winner

1973- NCAA Basketball Tournament Most Outstanding
      Player

1974- First Team College All-American

1974- College Player of the Year

1974- Naismith Award Winner

1977- NBA Finals Most Valuable Player

1978- NBA Most Valuable Player

1986- NBA Sixth Man Award

1993- Elected to Naismith Memorial Hall-of-Fame

1996- NBA 50th Anniversary 50 Greatest Players of All-Time

*Walton goes up for
a rebound.*

SOCIAL MISFIT?

Bill Walton drew much public criticism for his anti-Vietnam
War activities and other social commentary during the early
1970s.

Bill also has a philosophy on the role of athletics in society.
Sports as he sees them are "a means of drawing people
from different backgrounds closer together, a means of
having fun, and a means of promoting better health—for the
masses, not just the few." Adding, "Since the people who are
associated with the big business elements of sports are
calling the shots right now, changes are going to come
slowly."

Walton driving to the basket.

Moses
Malone

On any given night in the NBA there are more shots missed than those that are made. This fact places a high importance on another basketball statistic known as the rebound. The big man under the 'boards' has the primary responsibility of retrieving that rebound and putting it in the basket on offense, or passing it off to a teammate heading toward the other end of the court. In the history of basketball there have been few men more adept at this duty than Moses Malone. In his 21 seasons as a professional, he bounced from team to team like so many of the off-target shots he collected. When his playing days were over, Moses was the league's all-time leader for Offensive Rebounds. On the other end of the floor, he ranks second.

Moses Eugene Malone was the child of two smaller than average-sized parents. His father, who separated from the family when Moses was very young, was five-feet, six-inches tall. Moses' mother, Mary, stands five-feet, two-inches in height. She raised her only son under less-than-ideal conditions in Petersburg, Virginia. Mary worked first in a nursing home and later at a supermarket, trying to provide "Sweet Moses" with the best life she could afford. "I know how hard I came up, so I didn't want him to," said Mary. By the time he was 12 years old, Moses stood six-feet, three-inches tall! "He always loved his basketball," Mary would say, "and that's what gave that boy his courage."

Moses was too big to play a fair game with friends his own age, so he often found himself scrapping against the older kids. In a short time, he would outgrow the older boys in the neighborhood as well. When he signed up to play in a local youth league, the organizers enacted a rule prohibiting Moses from playing the center position. At the age of 14, he set a goal to be the best high school player in the country before the end of his junior season. The Petersburg High School basketball coach remembers just what a special performer Moses was. "He was such a serious player. Worked hard in practice all the time. No goofing around . . . . Ain't seen nothin' like him before, ain't seen nothin' like him since." Moses led his high school team to 50 straight victories, two State High School Championships, and was named High School All-American in his senior season.

The Utah Stars of the ABA (American Basketball Association) signed Moses in 1974. He became the first player to bypass college and head directly from high school to the professional ranks. In his rookie season, Moses led the eight-year-old league in offensive rebounding. The next season, the Stars' organization was disbanded, and Moses joined the ABA's Spirit of St. Louis. It would be the league's final season, before folding and partially merging with the more established NBA.

Moses was drafted by the Portland Trail Blazers, signed with the Buffalo Braves, and was traded to the Houston Rockets after only five days in the NBA! In his six seasons with the Rockets, he won the NBA's MVP Award twice and was the league's leading offensive rebounder every year. In 1981, Moses carried the Rockets to the NBA Finals, where they were defeated by the Boston Celtics (4-2). His next career stop was with the Philadelphia 76ers, where he joined Julius Erving to form a potent inside-outside combination. In his first season with Philadelphia, he became the league's MVP for the third time. The 76ers won the NBA Championship that season, and the MVP of the NBA Finals was Moses Malone. He had proven that the ability to get the rebound was every bit as valuable as the ability to score.

PROFILE:
Moses Malone
Born: March 23, 1955
Height: 6' 10"
Weight: 260 pounds
Position: Center
College: Did not attend
Teams: Utah Stars (1974-1975), Spirits of St. Louis (1975-1976), Buffalo Braves (1976), Houston Rockets (1976-1982), Philadelphia 76ers (1982-1986), Washington Bullets (1986-88), Atlanta Hawks (1988-1991), Milwaukee Bucks (1991-1993), Philadelphia 76ers (1993-94), San Antonio Spurs (1994-95)

CHAMPIONSHIP
SEASONS

Moses Malone playing for the Utah Stars of the ABA.

1982-83
NBA Championship
Philadelphia 76ers (4)
vs. Los Angeles Lakers
(0)

MOSES SPEAKS

Moses Malone has been a quiet individual since his childhood. His shyness was accentuated by a broken front tooth and a habit of mumbling when called upon in the classroom. When speaking on the art of rebounding, however, he is quite articulate. "Height and good jumping ability are advantages in offensive rebounding, but they are by no means the only factors in becoming a good rebounder," Moses says. "Rebounding is a skill improved by these three ingredients: aggressiveness, positioning, and determination. A good way to get out of the habit of watching shots before going in for the rebound is to automatically think that every shot taken will be missed. This will force you to anticipate where you think the shot will come off the rim."

THE REBOUND'S EVOLUTION

Before the 1973-74 NBA season, statistics for rebounding were kept as a single category, accounting for both ends of the court. Since that time, they have been divided into offensive and defensive rebound totals. Moses Malone is the league's all-time leader in offensive rebounding. He ranks fifth on the list for total rebounds.

NBA LEADER BOARD

Offensive Rebounds:

Career:

Moses Malone	**6,731**
Robert Parish	4,556 (through 1995-96)
Buck Williams	4,282

Season:

Moses Malone, 1978-79	587
Moses Malone, 1979-80	573
Moses Malone, 1981-82	558

Game:

Moses Malone, February 11, 1982	**21**
Moses Malone, February 9, 1979	**19**
Dennis Rodman, March 4, 1992	18 (OT)
Charles Oakley, March 15,1986	18 (OT)

Moses with the 76ers.

Defensive Rebounds:

Career:

Robert Parish	10,070 (through 1995-96)
Moses Malone	**9,481**
Kareem Abdul-Jabbar	9,394

Total Rebounds:

Career:

Wilt Chamberlain	23,924
Bill Russell	21,620
Kareem Abdul-Jabbar	17,440
Elvin Hayes	16,279
Moses Malone	**16,212**

Moses drives to the basket.

Bill
Laimbeer

Popularity is not a prerequisite for becoming a championship big man in the NBA. Wilt Chamberlain often referred to himself as "Goliath," when commenting on the way basketball fans perceived him. In the case of Bill Laimbeer, perceptions of opposing players and fans alike reached a level that can only be described as pure hatred.

Unlike Wilt, who in 14 professional seasons never fouled out of a basketball game, Bill was frequently sighted for flagrant rule violations. Behind him, the Detroit Pistons became known as the league's "Bad Boys," and Bill was their leading "Villain." He wasn't fast, couldn't jump, and lacked the quickness necessary for blocking shots. Instead, he relied on his ability to intimidate. If there were a way of measuring such things, Bill would be the NBA's all-time leading irritant. For two straight seasons the "Villain" and his "Bad Boys" were also the finest team in basketball.

William Laimbeer Jr. was born in Boston, Massachusetts. He spent the bulk of his formative years in the well-to-do Chicago suburb of Clarendon Hills, Illinois. William Sr. was a wealthy business executive for the Owens-Illinois corporation. His only son would later claim to be "the only player in the NBA who makes less money than his father." When Bill reached his junior year in high school the family moved to a suburb of Los Angeles, California. Bill's interests included golf, catching lobsters off the pier, and playing basketball for the Palos Verdes High School team.

Upon graduation from high school, Bill's only ambition was to have fun. This flawed sense of values proved costly when he flunked out of Notre

Dame University after his freshman year. He spent two semesters at Owens Technical College in Toledo, Ohio, where he studied his way back to the Fighting Irish for his junior season. Under head coach Digger Phelps, Bill was little more than a bench player in his final two seasons of college eligibility. The team's national reputation, however, helped to ready him for the future. "Half the people hated us at Notre Dame, half the people loved us," Bill remembers. "So I was marginally prepared for what was going to happen when I got to the pros."

Getting to the pros did not mean the NBA when Bill finished his college career. He was drafted in the third-round by the Cleveland Cavaliers, but signed a one year contract to play for Brescia of the Italian Basketball League. "Italy was just what I needed," Bill said. "I wanted playing time. Sitting on the bench in Cleveland wouldn't have helped me." He joined the Cavaliers the next season, where his rebounding and ability to hit shots from the outside became immediately noticeable. Taking particular notice of his inside presence and outside range were the Detroit Pistons. They traded for Bill in 1982. The Pistons were a

team on the rise, led by their sensational rookie Isiah Thomas. By 1986, they had added Joe Dumars and a notorious defensive specialist named Dennis Rodman. The "Bad Boys" had arrived. Soon, Bill would be recognized by basketball fans around the globe for his distasteful style of play. In particular, opposing players loathed the way he would "flop" to the floor, drawing fouls with the slightest of contact. In contrast, his own offenses often included flailing elbows, or an occasional push in the back to thwart an easy layup. Whatever his methods, Bill was twice the league's leading rebounder, and holds the Pistons' all-time record in that category. Detroit's "Bad Boys" never won a popularity contest, but for two straight seasons they were NBA Champions.

PROFILE:
Bill Laimbeer
Born: May 19, 1957
Height: 6' 11"
Weight: 260 pounds
Position: Center
College: Notre Dame University
Teams: Cleveland Cavaliers (1980-1982), Detroit Pistons (1982-1993)

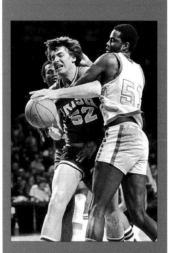

*Laimbeer with
Notre Dame.*

**1988-89
NBA Championship**
Detroit Pistons (4) vs.
Los Angeles Lakers (0)

**1989-90
NBA Championship**
Detroit Pistons (4) vs.
Portland Trail Blazers (1)

IRON MAN

Bill's ability to take punishment was as incredible as his willingness to dole it out. "Pain, injuries, that's all in the mind," he says. "You have to play through the pain and then the basketball takes over." If not for two separate one-game suspensions incurred for fighting, he may have easily set the NBA record for consecutive games played. They are the only two games he missed, during an 11 year time span!

THE ENTERTAINER

Bill Laimbeer seemed to enjoy the attention he received from the fans of opposing teams. "We are in the entertainment business," he said. "Make no mistake about that. If the fans in another town get off big time by coming and booing me all game long, that's what they pay their money for." Bill used this same line of thinking when defending his character. "I am not the mean, nasty, ugly person people make me out to be. I am a performer. I interject entertainment into the NBA's high wire act. That's my role. I am the heavy."

*Laimbeer plugging
up the middle.*

LAMB AND ZEKE

Bill's villainous reputation was a constant source of name-calling around the NBA. His detractors likened him to everything from a "street thug" to "pond scum." Meanwhile, his Piston teammates labeled their lionized leader as "Lamb." The nickname wasn't exactly true to character, but neither was his friendship with the team's offensive leader Isiah Thomas. Bill called Isiah "Zeke," and the two of them developed a lasting bond. Both had grown up in and around Chicago, but came from opposite poles of the socio-economic ladder.

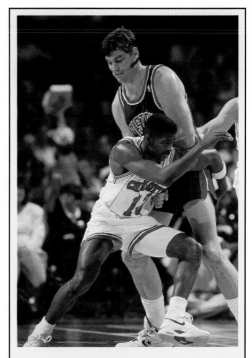

Laimbeer with the Pistons.

Even Zeke was not immune to the wrath of Lamb, however. In a scrimmage during the final season of their respective careers, one of Bill's flying elbows landed in Isiah's chest, cracking a rib. Their next altercation landed Isiah on the injured reserve. He broke his hand while punching Bill in the head! The second scrimmage skirmish, along with an aching back, caused Bill to consider his future. When Zeke returned from the disabled list, Lamb retired.

ATLANTA CHAIN-SAW-MASSACRE

Bill Laimbeer was unquestionably the most hated player in the NBA during his 14 seasons in the league. Patrick Ewing and Michael Jordan threw the only punches of their illustrious careers out of frustration over Bill's tactics. Fans at Atlanta's Omni Arena displayed their disdain for him on an evening billed as "Bill Laimbeer Night." At halftime of the Hawks/Pistons matchup, a wooden replica of Bill's blue uniform was brought out onto the floor. To the delight of 16,000 screaming fans, the duplicate was thrashed into sawdust with a chain saw!

Hakeem
Olajuwon

Since the days of the bespectacled George Mikan, *Big Men* have dominated the game of professional basketball. This is to take nothing away from players such as Larry Bird and Michael Jordan, who have led their teams to multiple NBA Championships without the existence of a dominating center in their lineup. In truth, it only enhances their legends as the premier players at their respective positions of forward and guard. It is their presence in the game's history that has helped to prevent superstar centers such as Patrick Ewing and David Robinson from attaining basketball's highest goal.

Another giant pivot-man, by the name of Shaquille O'Neal, currently awaits for his turn to lead the Los Angeles Lakers to a league title in the tradition of Wilt Chamberlain and Kareem Abdul-Jabbar. Shaq's first opportunity came in 1995, as a member of the Orlando Magic. The Houston Rockets defeated Orlando in the NBA Finals that season, as they had done to the New York Knicks in the previous season. The leader of the Rockets is a seven foot "Dream" from an island off the coast of Africa. His name is Hakeem Olajuwon.

Hakeem Abdul Ajibola Olajuwon was born in the busy merchant-town of Lagos, Nigeria. He grew up in a one story, three bedroom house with his mother, father, four brothers, and one sister. Hakeem's parents owned a concrete business in Lagos. They taught their children three family rules: study hard in

school, keep away from bad people, and always stay calm and collected.

Hakeem became acquainted with the game of basketball while attending the Moslem Teachers College. He was 15 years old and already six-feet, nine-inches tall. Prior to this time, his favorite sports had been soccer and team-handball. He began playing for the Lagos State junior basketball team in 1979, and led the team to a gold medal in the National All-Sports Festival. One year later, he joined Nigeria's junior national team. The 1980 All African Games were held in Casablanca, Morocco. With the support of his coach, Hakeem was asked to play for Nigeria's national men's team. With less than two years of experience on the basketball court, he had already reached the highest level of African competition.

By October of 1980, Hakeem had decided to seek his future fortune in America. He traveled to Houston, Texas, where he found a lasting new home. He studied business technology at the University of Houston, where he also learned the fundamentals of American college basketball. The Cougars advanced to the NCAA

Basketball Tournament's Final Four in each of Hakeem's three seasons with the team. He was named the tournament's MVP in 1983, despite a devastating last-second defeat in the championship game.

In the 1984 NBA Draft, Hakeem Olajuwon was the first player selected. The Houston Rockets chose him over a list of candidates that included Michael Jordan, Charles Barkley, and John Stockton. In his second professional season, the Rockets advanced to the NBA Finals, but were defeated by Larry Bird and the Boston Celtics. Then in 1994, with Bird retired and Jordan gone to pursue a career in baseball, Hakeem and the Rockets emerged as the best team in basketball. They won a second straight NBA Title in 1995, as Hakeem prevailed over Shaquille O'Neal, his heir apparent to the thrown of *Championship Big Men*.

PROFILE:
Hakeem Olajuwon
Born: January 21, 1963
Height: 7' 0"
Weight: 255 pounds
Position: Center
College: University of Houston
Teams: Houston Rockets (1984-)

CHAMPIONSHIP
SEASONS

Hakeem with the University of Houston.

1993-94
NBA Championship
Houston Rockets (4) vs. New York Knicks (3)

1994-95
NBA Championship
Houston Rockets (4) vs. Orlando Magic (0)

PHI SLAMMA JAMMA

Hakeem's freshman season at the University of Houston ended with a trip to the NCAA Final Four. The Cougars were defeated in the semifinal round by Michael Jordan's North Carolina team who went on to win the title. After the season, Hakeem was introduced to Moses Malone of the Houston Rockets. Moses befriended the young African transfer student, and the two engaged in a series of one-on-one matchups. When Hakeem returned as a sophomore he was in the best physical shape of his life.

The Cougars formed their own basketball fraternity that season, and nicknamed it the house of Phi Slamma Jamma. They were a high-flying, fast-breaking, slam-dunking powerhouse, piling up 25 straight victories and returning to the Final Four. Led by Hakeem "the Dream," and Clyde "the Glide" Drexler, Houston was the number one ranked team entering the tournament. This time they were beaten at the final buzzer by an overachieving North Carolina State team. Hakeem brought Houston back for a third straight time in 1984, but lost in the finals to Patrick Ewing and the Georgetown Hoyas.

Hakeem moves in for a layup.

CLASS REUNION

On the 10 year anniversary of their college championship matchup, Patrick Ewing and Hakeem Olajuwon faced-off in the 1994 NBA Finals. The Houston Rockets and New York Knicks battled for seven games before Houston eventually prevailed. Hakeem was named the tournament's MVP just as Patrick had been ten years earlier.

The next season brought a reunion for the house of Phi Slamma Jamma. Clyde Drexler came to the Rockets, teaming up with Hakeem to bring Houston a second-straight NBA Title. Hakeem set a new scoring record (131 pts.) for a four-game Final, and was named the MVP once again.

Hakeem slam dunks.

DREAM TEAM

The United States Olympic Basketball team became known as the "Dream Team" in 1992, when professional athletes were first allowed to compete. When Hakeem "the Dream" Olajuwon joined the team for the 1996 Olympic Games, the name took on a new meaning. Hakeem became an American citizen in 1993. Dream Team II brought home the gold medal just as their predecessors had done.

Hakeem goes to the hoop.

Glossary

All-American: A person chosen as the best amateur athlete at their position.

Assist: A pass of a basketball that enables a teammate to score.

Contract: A written agreement a player signs when they are hired by a professional team.

Dunk: To slam a ball through the basket from above.

Field Goal: In basketball, a converted shot worth either 2 or 3 points.

Final Four: The name given to the last four teams remaining in the NCAA college basketball championship tournament.

Foul: Illegal contact with another player. Basketball players are allowed a limited amount of fouls per game (usually 5 or 6).

Foul Out: To be put out of a game for exceeding the number of permissible fouls.

Free Throw: A shot taken while the game clock is stopped as a result of a foul by the opposing team, worth 1 point and taken from the free throw line.

Freshman: A student in the first year of a U.S. high school or college.

Junior: A student in the third year of a U.S. high school or college.

NCAA: An organization which oversees the administration of college athletics (National Collegiate Athletic Association).

NBA: An organization of professional basketball teams in North America (National Basketball Association).

Rebound: To retrieve and gain possession of the ball as it bounces off the backboard or rim after an unsuccessful shot.

Scholarship: A grant given to a student to pay for their college tuition.

Senior: A student in the fourth year of a U.S. high school or college.

Sophomore: A student in the second year of a U.S. high school or college.

Statistics: Numbers used to estimate a player's ability in different categories.

Varsity: The principal team representing a university, college, or school in sports, games, or other competitions.

Index

A

ABA (American Basketball Association) 7, 33
Alcindor, Lew 20, 21, 22
Atlanta Hawks 33
Auerbach, Red 9, 11, 24, 27

B

BAA (Basketball Association of America) 5
Barkley, Charles 41
Bird, Larry 25, 40, 41
Boston Celtics 9, 10, 13, 22, 24, 25, 26, 27, 28, 29, 30, 33, 41

C

Casablanca, Morocco 41
Cleveland Cavaliers 37
Cousy, Bob 9, 27
Creighton University 19

D

DeBusschere, Dave 17, 18
De Paul University 5, 6, 7
Detroit Pistons 36, 37, 38
Drexler, Clyde 43
Dumars, Joe 37

E

Erving, Julius 33
Ewing, Patrick 18, 39, 40, 42, 43

F

Florida State University 24, 25, 26
Frazier, Walt 18

G

Grambling State University 17

H

Harlem Globetrotters 13
Havlicek, John 9
Hayes, Elvin 23, 35
Heinsohn, Tommy 26, 27
Houston Rockets 30, 33, 40, 41, 42, 43

I

Italian Basketball League 37

J

Joliet, Illinois 4
Jones, K. C. 8, 27
Jordan, Michael 15, 39, 40

L

Lagos, Nigeria 40
Los Angeles Clippers 29
Los Angeles Lakers 10, 13, 14, 15, 18, 21, 22, 38, 40

M

McHale, Kevin 27
Milwaukee Bucks 21, 22, 25, 26, 27, 33
Minneapolis Lakers 4, 5, 6, 10
Monroe, Earl 18